Tonka® WORKING HARD WITH THE MIGHTY DUMP TRUCK™

Written by Justine Korman
Illustrated by Steven James Petruccio

SCHOLASTIC
New York Toronto London Auckland Sydney

ISBN 0-590-46481-7

Copyright © 1993 by Tonka Corporation.
All rights reserved. Published by Scholastic Inc.,
by arrangement with Tonka Corporation, 1027 Newport Avenue, Pawtucket, RI 02862.
THE MIGHTY TONKA is a trademark of Tonka Corporation.

12 11 10 9   5 6 7 8/9

Printed in the U.S.A.   24

First Scholastic printing, March 1993

Children's Room

Dan the Mighty Dump Truck driver gets an early start.
He and his dump truck have a busy day ahead.
First Dan makes sure the truck has a full tank of fuel.

Then Dan and the Mighty Dump Truck are on their way.
At this hour, other busy trucks are on the road, too.

Soon Dan arrives at the construction site.
Other trucks are already hard at work on a brand-new road.
Each one has a special job to do.

The bulldozer cuts the ground where it is too high
and fills it in where it is too low.
The backhoe digs up a small hill.

The loader piles dirt into the bed at the back of Dan's truck.
Load after load goes into the big bed.
The Mighty Dump Truck can hold a lot of dirt!

Dan drives to the other side of the construction site.
Dirt is needed there to fill in a ditch.
The Mighty Dump Truck's engine roars as it moves
the heavy load of dirt.

Dan works the controls in the dump truck's cab.
The front end of the truck bed lifts, and dirt pours out
the back. After many loads of dirt, the ditch is finally filled in.

Graders and bulldozers make the new road level, while Dan gets ready for the next job. A loader fills the Mighty Dump Truck's bed with stones.

Dan drives slowly along the new dirt road.
He lifts the Mighty Dump Truck's bed to pour out a
layer of stones. As the bed empties, the front end
lifts higher and higher.

A layer of sand will go on top of the stones.
A giant hopper pours sand into the big bed of Dan's
Mighty Dump Truck.

Dan carefully works the controls in the truck's cab to dump the sand on top of the stones.
Behind the truck a grader moves slowly along, leveling out the sand.

Now the new road is ready to be paved with asphalt.
And the truck drivers are ready for lunch.
Dan spots one of his favorite trucks — a hot dog truck!

After lunch, Dan's Mighty Dump Truck takes a load of
dirt to another construction site. Suddenly Dan hears
a siren wail.

He pulls over to the right side of the road to let two
fire trucks pass. One is the pumper truck.
The other carries the rescue ladders.

The fire chief's truck goes speeding by after the fire engines.
Dan doesn't mind pulling over for emergency vehicles.
Those trucks have an important job to do.

The Mighty Dump Truck is doing an important job, too.
The dirt it carries will help make the foundation for
a new apartment building where families will live.

Many trucks work together to put up a big building.
Dan's Mighty Dump Truck pours its load of dirt onto
the foundation while cranes, bulldozers, and excavators
lift, carry, and dig.

Dump trucks, big and small, bring in more and more dirt.
A sturdy building must have a firm foundation.

Soon it's time to mix concrete. Dan's Mighty Dump Truck dumps a load of sand into a huge cement mixer. The mixer spins the sand with gravel, cement, and water to make concrete.

When the concrete is ready, it is poured into the foundation.
The concrete will dry overnight.

At the end of the day, Dan drives home in his
Mighty Dump Truck. On the highway he passes big
delivery trucks and moving vans. Some of these trucks
will drive all night long.

But Dan and his Mighty Dump Truck need some rest.
Tomorrow will be another busy day!